To Lee and Diane

This book is set in Century 725/Monotype; Grilled Cheese BTN/Fontbros

Printed in Malaysia
Reinforced binding

First Edition, September 2007
30 29 28 27 26 25 24 23
FAC-029191-21008
Library of Congress Cataloging-in-Publication Data on file.

ISBN: 978-1-4231-0686-9

Visit www.hyperionbooksforchildren.com and www.pigeonpresents.com

There Is a Bird on Your Head!

An **ELEPHANT & PIGGIE** Book
By **Mo Willems**
Hyperion Books for Children / *New York*

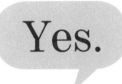

There is a bird
on my head?

9

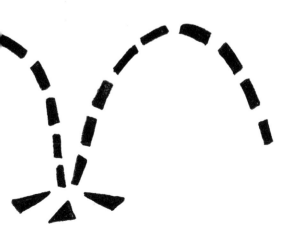

Is there a
bird on my
head now?

No.

Now there are two birds on your head.

They are
in love!

How do you know they are love birds?

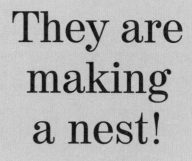

They are
making
a nest!

Two birds are making a nest on my head?

I am afraid to ask . . .

You have three eggs on your head.

Then I have good news!

The eggs are hatching!

They have
hatched.

Now, I have three baby chicks on my head!

I do not want three baby chicks, two birds, and a nest on my head!

Where do you want them?

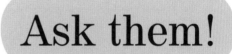

49

Have you read all of Elephant and Piggie's funny adventures?

Today I Will Fly!

My Friend Is Sad

I Am Invited to a Party!

There Is a Bird on Your Head!
(Theodor Seuss Geisel Medal)

I Love My New Toy!

I Will Surprise My Friend!

Are You Ready to Play Outside?
(Theodor Seuss Geisel Medal)

Watch Me Throw the Ball!

Elephants Cannot Dance!

Pigs Make Me Sneeze!

I Am Going!

Can I Play Too?

We Are in a Book!
(Theodor Seuss Geisel Honor)

I Broke My Trunk!
(Theodor Seuss Geisel Honor)

Should I Share My Ice Cream?

Happy Pig Day!

Listen to My Trumpet!

Let's Go for a Drive!
(Theodor Seuss Geisel Honor)

A Big Guy Took My Ball!
(Theodor Seuss Geisel Honor)

I'm a Frog!

My New Friend Is So Fun!

Waiting Is Not Easy!
(Theodor Seuss Geisel Honor)

I Will Take a Nap!

I *Really* Like Slop!

The Thank You Book